Lyman H. Sproull

Snowy Summits

A collection of western poems

Lyman H. Sproull

Snowy Summits
A collection of western poems

ISBN/EAN: 9783337255961

Printed in Europe, USA, Canada, Australia, Japan

Cover: Foto ©Andreas Hilbeck / pixelio.de

More available books at **www.hansebooks.com**

SNOWY SUMMITS.

A COLLECTION OF

WESTERN POEMS

BY

LYMAN H. SPROULL,

AUTHOR OF

"LINES BY LAMPLIGHT," "CAMP AND COTTAGE,"

—

ST. LOUIS
A. R. FLEMING PRINTING CO.,
1898.

PREFACE.

IN PRESENTING this collection of poems to the friendly public, the author trusts that he has succeeded in truthfully portraying the subjects of his verse. The scout, the echoes, the Indian, the nameless grave, and the magpie in the cotton-wood, are among the many familiar sights and sounds which make dear to his heart the land of snowy peaks, the majestic precipices, and the rugged slopes which go to make up the great chain of the Rocky Mountains.

L. H. S.

CRIPPLE CREEK, COLO., July, 1897.

CONTENTS.

vii

CONTENTS.

CONTENTS.

I.

Snowy Summits.

SNOWY SUMMITS.

PRELUDE.

Are you sick of rush and sweat,
  Where the soul must ever cry?
Are you sick with fear and fret;
  Are you weary?—so am I!

Let us steal to Nature's lap—
  She alone can sympathize—
And as children for their nap,
  Close in rest our dreamy eyes,

With that night of dusky hair
  O'er our slumbering faces spread—
Till the fair surpasses fair,
  And our fears are comforted.

Thus with glowing, wind-kissed cheeks,
  In our dreams so sweetly odd,
Let us seek the snowy peaks
  Sheltered by the peace of God.

13

SUMMER CLOUDS.

The high aerial fleet floats on
   In proud and silent majesty;
Bright elfin barks returning home
   Across the dark blue, welkin sea.

Far up the mountain slope the dim,
   Sweet troop of shadows follow slow,
And marks the moving ships which limn
   Their number on the world below.

The breath of heaven is in each sail,
   And on their decks the smile of day,
While at their prows the azure veil
   Of distance blends to airy spray.

On past the dark terrestrial shoal,
   To where discordant troublings cease,
They bear some fair, unfettered soul,
   To realms of beauty and of peace.

Now far within the evening pink,
   They pause and mingle in retreat,
And seem to slip behind the brink
   Of ocean mystical and sweet.

So, fading from the world and me,
  They pass to realms of peace and dreams,
And leave upon the ethereal sea
  No wake among the wavy beams.

THE STATIONED SCOUT.

High on the bold, gray granite shelf
  He builds his cabin, bleak and lone,
Where eagles well might covet it
  As in an eyrie of their own.

Here from his station on the height
  He views the land far, far below,
And sees where slopes of piñon green
  Reach upward, ending in the snow.

With pipe and glass, and dog and gun,
  Companions of the plain and wood,
He sits and scans the broken peaks,
  Which breathe of peace and solitude.

All thro' the quiet night he hears
    The weird and lonely owlet hoots;
And at the dawn afar appears
    The smouldering camp-fire of the Utes.

The blazing disk of morning sun
    Across the plains, a burning flood,
Lights up his low and dingy room,
    And paints old Baldy's head with blood.

He sees far on the plains below,
    With distant hazy dreams endowed,
Each patch of moving buffalo,
    So like the shadow of a cloud.

Thro' all the heat of summer day,
    Each change, each object on the plain,
Or in the hills, arrests his eye,
    Until the shadows grow again.

He sees the western sun sink low,
    To hide behind the neighboring peaks,
Which feed from fields of shining snow
    The babbling fountains of the creeks.

And then at night the campers' light
  Comes dimly on the distant plain,
Which brings to him in memories bright
  The days of roving youth again.

He sees the crescent 'mid the rift
  Of nightly clouds, in tranquil light,
Back down along the notched clift
  To bid the world and him good-night.

THE ECHOES.

Morning sets the echoes ringing
  Thro' the sunny hills of day:
    Die away—Die away.
Many fade while others, bringing
Sweet replies of youthful singing,
    Die away.
While the ringing still keeps ringing
  Thro' the bright and dewy May:
    Die away—Die away.

2

Midday keeps the echoes flying
   Strong and hopeful, wild and gay:
   Die away—Die away.
Others come while they are dying,
Coming, calling, ever crying,
     Die away.
Still replying, keep replying
   Thro' the vaulted skies of day:
   Die away—Die away.

Now the echoes all are meeting
   In the evening, soft and gray:
   Die away—Die away.
While the feeble heart is beating
With this one continuous greeting,
     Die away.
Still repeating, still repeating,
   Where the fitful shadows play:
   Die away—Die away.

THE BRAVE'S RETURN.

———

The river is soft with that holy light
Which comes from the queen of the silent
    night—
       A returning brave
       From the battle's rave,
In his bark canoe on the moonlit wave,
Is gliding along o'er the waters bright.

The mountains, far in the distant west,
Outlined on the cold blue, starry breast
       Of a midnight sky,
       Rise dark and high,
Like sentries over the hills which lie
Along the river in tranquil rest.

The boat is moored by the moonlit sand,
And the bush is parted with wary hand,
       Till a path is found
       On the damp, cold ground,
Which leads the brave with a joyous bound
To the hidden home of his native land.

Two eyes peep in where the soft moonlight
Steals down thro' the tent from the silent
    night;
       And there she lies
       With her dark, deep eyes,
Unconscious quite of the starry skies,
But wide awake to a vision bright.

A dusky form from the dewy vines,
Steals out from the shadows among the pines,
       Like a spirit strayed
       From the mystic shade
Of the Hunting Ground, to again invade
The happy haunt where his love reclines.

The hills are silent; the wood is bright;
And the boat still rides in the soft moonlight;
       While thro' the rent
       In the hemlock tent,
The gaze of the heavenly stars is bent
On the brave who dreams with his love
    to-night.

MAGGIE OF THE ARKANSAW.

———

Maggie from her cotton-wood,
  Young and helpless, watched the quiver
  Of the sunset on the river,
  Dying to a dusky shiver
As the shadows veiled the flood.

There she saw the day depart
  From her nest, and yawned and spluttered,
  As she closed her eyes and muttered
  Many gratitudes, which fluttered
From her overflowing heart.

When the morning came again,
  Maggie turned her eyes as ever
  On the rolling of the river,—
  Which would dimple, ripple, quiver,
With the wind and with the rain.

When at last the fall-winds raw,
  Woke the willows with their sighing,
  Maggie, screaming, laughing, crying,
  Went a-shooting and a-flying
Up and down the Arkansaw.

THE SHADOWS.

Slowly the shadows creep
　　Down from the peaks;
Down from the woody steep,
　　Over the creeks;
Painting　on　pasture　lands　sombresome
　　streaks.

　　Out from the spruce they come,
　　　　Out from the mill;
　　Born of the setting sun,
　　　　Silent and still;
Stretching and reaching out over the hill.

　　Stately and column-wise,
　　　　Slender and tall,
　　Sweetly they solemnize
　　　　Barnside and wall,
While in the dusty lane, broken they fall.

　　Over the sandy plain,
　　　　Over the farms,
　　Back to the night again,
　　　　Back to its arms;
Back to its silence, and back to its charms.

DREAMS OF THE FALL.

I.

Distance so mellow,
Hazy and blue;
Aspens in yellow,
Mornings in dew;

Clouds in the heaven
Scattered like fleece;
Sounds in the even
Muffled with peace;

Nothing to cumber—
Dreams of the fall—
Beauty and slumber
Rest over all.

II.

Here in touch with Nature, dreaming,—
Dreaming by the smoky streams,
We can watch the sunset gleaming
Softly over scattered dreams.

Dreams are lingering in the grasses;
  Dreams are lingering in the pines;
Dreams are lingering in the voices
  Of the cool, crisp, mountain winds.

Here the magpies' notes are calling,
  Calling wildly, loudly, sad;
And the leaves are falling, falling,
  Red and yellow, gold and red.

Dreams are lingering in the blossoms
  Faded by the upland glade;
Dreams are lingering in the sunlight;
  Dreams are lingering in the shade.

Sharp and chill the wind is breathing,—
  Breathing over distant peaks,
Where belated birds are leaving
  Cañon, crag, and frosty creeks.

Dreams are lingering in verdure
  Bitten by the early frost;
Dreams are lingering in the thickets,
  Where the tomtit's cry is lost.

Here we see the hills of autumn,
  And the vales which intervene;
And the pine-trees and the aspen—
  Yellow patches mixed with green.

Dreams of beauty linger with us,
  On the hills and by the streams;
Dreams of God and dreams of Nature,—
  Ever-blessed, peaceful dreams!

III.

Distance so mellow,
  Hazy and blue;
Aspens in yellow,
  Mornings in dew;

Brooklets all smoky,
  Freighted with leaves;
Cañons so moky
  Which silence retrieves;

Nothing to cumber—
  Dreams of the fall—
Beauty and slumber
  Rest over all.

THE WILLOW BY THE WINDOW.

Denuded by the wind and frost,
 The lonely willow lifts its arms,
As if in prayer for something lost—
 The beauty of its summer charms.

Alone, a picture of distress,
 It bends and bows to every gust,
Which jeers its trembling nakedness,
 And soils it branches with the dust.

And on the frosty window-pane,
 At early morning, cold and clear,
I see its ghostly arms again,
 As painted by the atmosphere.

Ah, mourner, there shall come a day,
 When freed from frost and wind's demean,
The sweet and tender, budding May
 Shall give thee back thy robes of green!

THE ROSE AT SUNSET.

———

That fading light low in the west
    Is but the parting smile of day,
Which, resting on the mountain crest,
    Puts on a countenance of gray.

The rose has caught the last faint blush
    Of sunset on her tender cheek,
And drops to sleep within the hush
    Of this great shadow of the peak;

While folded in her kindly breast
    There lies a drop of evening dew—
So like a tear her heart has blessed
    For some dear soul she loved and knew.

— — ——

THE EMIGRANT'S CHILD.

———

Far out in the hush of the mountain land
    There lies the grave of a little child;
Unwept by heart and untended by hand—
    Alone with the grass and the aspen wild.

It was years ago—so the story goes—
  When the "Fifties" rang with the tales of
     gold,
That they laid her there, 'mid the falling
    snows,
  To sleep alone in the damp and cold.

What mother sobbed with the pangs of woe,
  What father grieved as he urged his teams,
Tradition tells not, and we only know
  That the child is there in a land of dreams.

It was just last year, when I passed that way,
  I saw o'er the mound in the bushes low,
A bird had erected her nest to stay
  And sing to the soul of the sleeper below·

ALL DAY.

All day the mantling mist has wrapped
  The peaks about the town;
All day the weeping clouds have dropped
  Their tears of sorrow down.

All day within this lonely room
  My thoughts played hide and seek,
As children thro' the mist and gloom,
  Who would not smile or speak.

All day these dripping eaves have kept
  My soul awake to pray
For these dear ones, that have but wept,
  All day—all day—all day.

II.

Silva.

SILVA.

THE MYSTIC OCEAN.

Once, deep in a dream's creation,
  Swept a dark blue, mystic ocean,
Splashing on the far horizon,
  At the sky-wall of its waters.

Stars hung o'er it in the twilight;
  Moons hung o'er it in the midnight;
Suns hung o'er it in the daylight;
  Rainbows spanned it in the morning;
Rainbows spanned it in the evening;
  Clouds went drifting high above it,
While the whispering winds caressed it,
  Wooed its waves and sought its border.

And these fairy moons went drifting
  Thro' the sky in all directions;
North to south, 'mid starry bowers,
  West to east; there fading softly

To dim, flickering lights, suspended
   Like so many fairy lanterns,
O'er the dark and dreamy ocean.

   And these fairy suns would cluster
In the vaulted skies of heaven,
   Shedding soft and silvery arrows
Down upon the world beneath them.

II.
THE BLACK FOREST.

In the middle of this ocean,
   Growing from a sunken island,
Was a forest, black as midnight,
   Casting shadows deep and silent
O'er the wrinkling world of waters;
   Where the floating clouds around it,
Drifting thro' the gloom and silence,
   Broke upon the lone and sombre
Wall of this great wood enchanted.

Massive tree-trunks, which would measure
   Many miles in their circumference,
Stood amid the floating mosses—
   In the midnight, reaching upward,

Leagues and leagues until their topmost
  Branches brushed the clouds which floated
'Neath the moons and stars of heaven.

From the skies, in all directions,
  Came the ocean, rolling, racing,
Breaking high in many voices
  Thro' the night of massive tree-trunks;
Where the echoes, weird and dreary,
  Answered back the ceaseless slapping
Of the waves throughout the darkness.

III.

SILVA.

This was Silva:—this great forest;
  This strange continent of tree-tops;
This black wood of dreamy echoes—
  Rooted in the slime of midnight,
With its top-boughs tipped with sunlight,
  Tipped with moonlight, tipped with star-
      light;
This great wilderness, whose branches
  Crossed and recrossed thro' the darkness,
With its sombre leaves and mosses,
  Like dark, massive clouds suspended.

IV.
FIRST SETTLERS OF SILVA.

In across the silent ocean,
　From the distant land of Nowhere,
Came a band of elfin people—
　Funny featured little creatures—
To this oceanic forest.

Landing on the mossy islands,
　Floating thro' the one continuous
Midnight, with their many candles
　Gleaming strangely thro' the darkness—
Like a swarm of fire-flies gathered—
　They erected miles of ladders
Up the gloomy tree-trunks, reaching
　Into many sunny sections
Of this dark and mossy region.

Finding in their upper Silva
　Many bright and pleasant places,
They called other elfins to them
　In across the world of waters;
Bringing in their ships of silver,
　Cattle, chickens, dogs and ponies,
That would climb the curious ladders
　With their little elfin masters.

V.

BUILDING HAMLETS AND HIGHWAYS.

———

Here these queer, industrious people,
　In the sunlit parts of Silva,
Far above the inky darkness,
　Hewed broad highways round the tree-
　　trunks,
And along the giant branches;
　Built their swinging bridges, reaching
Out from limb to limb, connecting
　All the parts of their dominion.

Then they built their silvan hamlets;
　Hewed their avenues thro' mosses,
Round their markets and their dwellings;
　Made their little parks in shady
Nooks, and raised their odd pavilions,
　Where the fountains, fed from lakelets
Of the dew upon the foliage,
　Sparkled in the mellow sunlight.

VI.
THE KING OF SILVA.

———

Halo was the King of Silva,
    And he loved his people dearly,
Who erected him a palace
    Near the border of the forest—
In the brightest, highest tree-top,
    Reached by one long, winding highway,
Like a serpent round the tree-trunk.

Here he viewed his queer dominion
    Daily from his odd piazza,
Where the leaves and creepers mingled.
    Miles and miles below him wrinkled
The great ocean which went quivering,
    Moaning, splashing thro' the tree-trunks,
Down in that continuous midnight.

VII.
THE CHILDREN OF SILVA.

———

Tiny children raced the pathways
    With their jumping-ropes and playthings—
Swinging in the tangled grape-vines;
    Hanging over dim abysses;

Clambering down in excavations
  Of the knots, or shouting wildly
When they gained some sunny leaflet,
  Over which they romped and rambled.

Sun-tanned youths and rosy maidens,
  Filling all the leaves with laughter,
Strayed away to backwood corners
  Of the forest, with their baskets
And their prankish little horses—
  Loading them with nuts and berries,
Grapes and apples, which they gathered.

VIII.

THE PACK-PONIES.

Ah, how sweet to watch them coming!
  These dear, faithful little ponies—
Stringing out along the branches,
  Down the twigs along the pathways;
Rounding knots and jumping hillocks
  Of the bark, o'erlaid with mosses—

All in line with bells and bridles—
    One beneath a mammoth apple;
One beneath a nut or berry;
    Others laden with the sirups
Gathered from the sprays of maple.

Out across the swinging bridges,
    Where the twilight depths beneath them
Lay serene as bay or lakelet;
    Out along the winding highways,
Round the tree-trunks, hastening homeward
    To some little silvan village.

IX.

EVENING AT SILVA.

When the evening came with rainbows
    Shining forth in all directions,
Halo watched the north-moons rising
    Slowly o'er his leafy kingdom—
Floating southward o'er the tree-tops,
    Till they passed his silvan palace,
And at last, in southern heavens,
    Dwindled down to stars and vanished.

Then the west-moons, which belated
  In their trip across the heavens,
Came on faster than the others;
  Sailing high above the ruler,
Drifting eastward; dying softly
  To wee, gleaming lights which hovered
Just above the east horizon,
  Where the sky and ocean mingled.

X.

TWILIGHT AT SILVA.

———

When at last the moons had vanished,
  Or had faded to a glimmer,
And the twilight darkened softly,
  Like a veil of peace descending,
Halo watched the lights which twinkled
  Like the million stars of heaven,
From the many rural hamlets
  Scattered thro' the leafy country,
Where his people in their houses,
  Played their games and sang rejoicing.

XI.

MORNING AT SILVA.

———

When the morning came, and many
    Sunken suns came climbing upward,
Or appeared thro' depths of azure,
    Casting many quivering arrows
Thro' the airy territory,
    Halo listened to the crowing
Of the many cocks, which sounded
    Faint and dreamy in the distance;
Or the barking of some startled
    Dog that heard the early rumble
Of some elfin farmer's wagon,
    As it rattled down the branches,
Out upon the wooden roadway.

XII.

DAY AT SILVA.

———

Thro' the sunny day King Halo
    Watched the many winding highways,
Lined with people and with ponies
    Going to and from the hamlets,

Where they bartered at their markets.
  Here and there were droves of cattle,
Flocks of chickens, bands of ponies,
  High on sunny leaves which shaded
Other droves and bands commingling
  On the lower leaves and branches,
Where the tinkling bells awakened
  Echoes thro' the night below them.

Thus the ruler watched, delighted
  With his busy little people;
Watched them coming, watched them going;
  Climbing up the leafy pathways;
Traveling on the wooden highways;
  Crossing on the swinging bridges;
Drinking at the sparkling fountains;
  Bartering at the shady markets;
Dancing in the queer pavilions;
  Singing in their rosy parlors;
Playing games and making merry,
  In this elfin land of Silva.

III.

Interludes.

INTERLUDES.

THE CLOUDS.

The skies are filled with clouds of gray;
  Down on my heart the sunshine lies.
  Ah! what care I for outer skies,
Or clouds that may infest the day,
  While my soul sleeps in paradise—
  In Hope's sweet paradise?

Where are the clouds of yesterday?
  I cannot see them in the sky.
Alas! they have not fled away!
  Down on my weary heart they lie
In banks of dark and chilly gray—
In banks of sullen gray.

47

INTERRUPTED DREAMS.

I.

Soul, I am weak and weary;
　Soul, thou hast eyes to see,
Look thro' the veil of slumber,
　Speak thro' thy love to me:

What are these voices saying?—
　Sad and discordant sounds
Out in the darkness straying—
　Out where the gloom abounds.

II.

Only the wind complaining;
　Only the pine's reproof;
Only the night-cloud raining
　Over the cabin roof;

Only the herd intoning
　Out by the lonely shed;
Only the river moaning
　Over its gravel-bed.

III.

Down in the depths of slumber
  Visions will brighten there;
Brighten with naught to cumber—
  Fancies so sweet and fair.

Now to my eyes are dawning
  Sights which my boyhood knew;
Sights which were bathed in sunshine,
  Sights which were bathed in dew:

Here is the school-room holding
  Squares of the midday sun;
Here are the whispering scholars,
  And here are the cobwebs spun;

Here is the teacher standing;
  Down to her desk she goes,
Glancing with looks of kindness
  Over her drowsy rows.

Here are the prairies sleeping
  Sweet in their summer dream;
Here are the flowers peeping
  Up by the babbling stream;

4

Here are the cooling shadows,
  Cast by the willow-trees,
Out on the scented meadows,
  Filled with the droning bees;

Here are the grape-vines clinging
  To oaks which are tall and fair;
Here is the redbreast singing
  Songs on the fragrant air;

Here are the locusts whirring
  Out from the maple-trees;
Here are the tree-tops stirring,
  Filled with the summer breeze;

Here are the wild oats waving
  Over the prairie lands;
Here are the flowers nodding,
  Tempting our childish hands.

Why do these visions waver,
  Brighten, to soon depart?
What are these discords entering
  In at my trembling heart?

IV.

Only the dark cloud scowling
Out in the moonlight wane;
Only a lone wolf howling
Over the lonely plain;

Only the echoes dying
Down on the cliffs afar;
Only a night-hawk flying
Out in the murky air.

V.

Sleep while the soul is dreaming;
  Sleep while the night is here;
Sleep while the stars are gleaming
  Down thro' the heavens clear.

Here are the wheat fields waving,—
  Billowy seas of green;
Here are the tall groves standing
  Out in the sunset sheen;

Here are the corn fields nodding,
  Decked in their silks and leaves;
Here are the stacks and stubbles,
  And here are the scattered sheaves;

Here are the threshers singing
　　Out on the wind-swept plain;
Here are the wagons stringing
　　In with their loaded grain;

Here are the cattle lowing
　　Down by the pasture bars;
Here are the milkers going
　　Under the early stars;

Here thro' the drove of bossies—
　　Lulled by a tinkling bell—
Swiftly the fire-fly carries
　　Light to the lonely dell;

Here comes the sweet and mellow
　　Voice of the whip-poor-will,
Floating in waves of music
　　Out on the silent hill;

Here are the pathways leading
　　Home—to the home of yore—
Home to the heart of mother;
　　Home to the cottage door.

Why are these visions fading,—
  Fading before my eyes?
Why are my fancies flitting,
  Now as the sweet dream dies?

Why has my soul awakened,
  Startled as if in fear?
What are these sounds which gather
  Now on my wary ear?

VI.

Only the wind complaining;
  Only the pine's reproof;
Only the night-cloud raining
  Over the cabin roof;

Only the echoes playing
  Out where the mountains stand;
Only the spirit straying
  Out of a promised land.

THE CLOCK OF LIFE.

Life is going
All unknowing—
Rivers flowing
    On and on.
Hopes are waning;
Life's complaining:
Time gone—Time going—
Time going—Time gone.

Love is calling,
Leaves are falling,
Winds appalling,
    Grieve our home.
Hearts are beating,
Love's repeating,
Calling, come: Come, calling:
Come, calling: Calling, come.

Time is flying,
Night is hieing,
Day is dying,
    Sad and wan.

Hopes are waning;
Life's complaining:
Time gone—Time going—
Time going—Time gone.

Love is sleeping,
Eyes are weeping,
Age is creeping
   Up anon.
Hearts are beating,
Love's repeating,
Calling, come: Come, calling:
Come, calling: Calling, come.

Dreams are passing,
Winds harassing,
Clouds amassing
   At the dawn.
Hope is waning;
Life's complaining:
Time gone—Time going—
Time going—Time gone.

Death is seizing,
Life's uneasing,
Lips are freezing,
    Kissed and gone.
Hearts are beating,
Love's repeating,
Calling, come: Come, calling:
Come, calling: Calling, come.

A PLEA FOR PEACE.

Oh Trouble, why trouble you me?
    The day it is balmy and bright;
Keep out of its sweetness for me;
    Keep out of the softness of night.

Keep out of my heart, my heart;
    Keep out of my ear, my ear;
For I feel in the depth of my soul
    That the spirit of peace is here.

So Trouble, don't trouble you me,
  For the world is as happy as fair;
Ah Trouble, keep out of my eyes;
  Keep off from the brown of my hair.

The clouds of the night are not sad,
  And the winds are suggestive of mirth;
So Trouble, away from my door,
  While the darkness is over the earth.

The past is forgotten and gone,
  And the future is nobly planned;
So Trouble, keep out of my heart,
  While the sunshine is over the land.

The mountains are dancing in light;
  Or clothed in that mystical blue;
Or wrapped in the dreaming of night;
  Forgetful, oh Trouble, of you.

Keep out of my way, my way;
  Keep out of my sight, my sight;
Oh Trouble, keep out of my day;
  Oh Trouble, keep out of my night.

The leaves are all dancing with joy,
  While the winds of the valley are free;
And I live in the strength of their love;
  So Trouble, why trouble you me?

What matter, tho' love is a pain!
  There 're times when the saddest are gay;
And mine will be coming again—
  So Trouble, keep out of my way.

There is love in the musical wind;
  There is beauty in every place;
So Trouble, keep out of my mind;
  So Trouble, keep out of my face.

Keep out of the peace of my breast;
  Keep out of the ring of my laugh;
Oh Trouble, keep out of my rest;
  Oh Trouble, keep out of my path.

I'm still in the morning of life,
  With a soul that's unhampered and free;
And my hopes are as strong as my love—
  So Trouble, why trouble you me?

What matter, tho' tears I have shed;
  What matter, tho' pains I have borne?
They are over—all over and gone;
  So Trouble, keep out of the morn.

The sunset is flashing with gold,
  And the wind has forgotten to grieve;
Ah Trouble, keep out of their hold;
  Ah Trouble, keep out of the eve.

And Trouble, keep out of my plans;
  Keep out of my soul, my soul;
Keep out of my heart, my hands;
  Oh Trouble, keep out of the whole.

For life is not worthless nor wrong,
  If hopeful and earnest I be;
And my heart is as willing as strong—
  So Trouble, why trouble you me?

IV.

Quatrains and Pentastichs.

QUATRAINS.

TO THE GOLD SEEKER.

———

Before you throw your float away,
  Go break it—look it thro' and thro';
For hidden in its gloom and gray,
  There may be specks of gold for you.

A SMILE.

———

A smile is but the blossom of a thought;
  A bud, concealed in some secluded place
Amid a million buds, which caught
  A ray of light and blossomed on the face.

AMBITION.

———

Place high your mark and shoot away,
  Although the arrows fall;
We always get a little done
  By striving after all.

TO-DAY.

———

Let's build to-day what our to-day demands,
  And let to-morrow's stone be laid to-
    morrow;
This wall of life erected by our hands,
  Should grow but as we grow, in joy or
    sorrow.

THE TRUE MAN.

———

I love the man who, speaking to a friend,
  Finds time to place a good word for his
    wife;
And thro' the conversation to the end,
  Shows love for those who help to bless his
    life.

LIFE'S QUEST.

———

A miner, searching all his life for gold,
  In dark and diverse places, ill at ease,
Looked o'er an autumn forest, and behold!
  His life-long quest was shining on the
    trees!

THE CLIFF DWELLER.

High on the cliff where sunset fancies throng,
  We find the notchèd sticks where once he
    clomb
To where his loved ones met him with a
    song,
  Which still, I fancy, fills his ruined home.

AT THE RUINS.

Where once a happy life thronged thro' the
    door,
  And filled with song and laughter every
    room,
We now have dust and mummies on the floor;
  Together with the mystery and the gloom.

UNOPENED HISTORY.

A history sleeps within this air profound,
  Which still remains unopened unto man;
All clasped in golden silence, stitched and
    bound
  By all the prayers of that vanished clan.

THE TERRESTRIAL HOUSEHOLD.

———

The evening winds has snuffed at last the
    candle of the day,
While lie the sunset embers on the hearth-
    stone of the west;
Down from the welkin curtains with a soft
    and soothing ray,
The stars smile o'er the household of hu-
    manity at rest.

- - -

AN OCTOBER EVENING.

———

Now the hazy hills of lazy autumn whisper
    of October,
While the tinted peaks seem printed on
    the evening, faintly bright,
And the lonely plains tell only of a life that's
    weird and sober,
As the hunter's moon goes drifting thro'
    the bosom of the night.

PERSEVERANCE.

———

Work on, dejected fashioner,
  In crude, though honest art;
A simple tear is no disgrace
  When coming from the heart.

LEAVES OF LIFE.

———

Our life is but a book of leaves;
  We turn one over—call it new;
But soon 'tis soiled, and sadly grieves
  Our heart as much as past ones do.

--

HOPES.

———

How quick the step, when lie ahead
  The prospects of an earthly gain;
How slow the step when, cold and dead,
  Such hopes are numbered with the slain.

THE SINGING CONES.

While straying thro' the mountain pines,
  I gathered up some scattered cones,
And pointing them toward the winds,
  They sang to me in elfin tones.

THE SEED.

Why should the seed cling to the winter
    clod
  Thro' every dark and cold and stormy
    hour?
Ah, friends, within its silent bosom, God
  Has placed a soul to blossom in a flower.

KANSAS.

All high and dry beneath the glare of many
    suns,
  It sleeps where once there ran a dark and
    slimy sea;
Its chalky beds, its rocks, and fossil skele-
    tons,
  Tell what its life has been—but not what
    it may be.

HIDDEN QUALITIES.

———

'Tis only as we burnish stone
  We find its polished worth;
'Tis only as we question souls
  That knowledge cometh forth.

——— — —.

FROM THE GLOOM.

———

The purest diamond ever grows
  In places dark and narrow;
So, oft the sweetest thoughts are those
  Which come from depths of sorrow.

——— — .——

THE RIGHT TO DREAM.

———

If we can't be the stars above,
  In magnitude to beam like them,
We have a right their light to love,
  And as admirers, dream of them.

NINE O'CLOCK.

The heavens are arched by the Milky-way;
　The crescent is hung in a western pine;
The Pleiades blink in the orient gray,
　And the Dipper is up to the mark of nine.

THE CAMPERS.

Where night o'ertakes them there they make
　　a home,
　And while the camp-fire paints their grimy
　　cheeks,
They listen to the music of the pines,
　Or watch the moon drift over distant peaks.

MIDNIGHT.

When midnight crowns the silent peaks
　　around
　With sinking stars and moon with placid
　　light,
How sweet to dream of God's untrodden
　　ground,
　And listen to the voices of the night.

ANOTHER DAY.

When Sol peeps in upon the brightening
    slope
  Of silent forests, tipped with silvery ray,
He sees a world of dreamy eyes which ope
  Upon the morning of another day.

THE CITIZEN.

Man loves his country as he loves his wife,
  His children, and the comforts of his home;
If he cares little for his own in life,
  He cares still less for what's his country's
    doom.

THE SOLDIER.

The soldier who proved truest in the field,
  Was he, who, back of powder, shell and
    ball,
Had dear ones in his home who daily kneeled
  For one who fought to save their little all.

THE BIGOT.

The bigot thinks that he of course is right,
    And when another cannot see as he,
He says, "Poor soul! he has not seen the
      light."
The other says, "As dark as he can be!"

THE OLD AND THE NEW.

What seemed a truth but yesterday
    Has faded now to specter wan;
Another day with brighter ray
    Has brought a new truth with the dawn.

REQUIREMENTS.

If earth did not require a light,
    We should not have a sun;
If man did not require a God,
    He would not think of One.

DARK THOUGHTS.

As stealthy rats that gnaw the grain at night,
  If undisturbed will make their nests in it;
So these dark thoughts, if never put to flight,
  Will gnaw the heart, till ruin rests in it.

THE TOWER.

On solid rock, which ocean billows chafe,
  In darkest night amid the seething strife,
It stands erect and holds that lamp of faith
  Above the dark and stormy sea of life.

FROM DARKNESS TO LIGHT.

The one who weeps the most forlorn at night,
  And grieves that clouds are hovering o'er
    his way,
May be the first to hail the breaking light,
  And bask in beams of Truth's eternal day.

THE SPHERE OF MAN.

'Tis no disgrace to the worm to crawl,
　But mimic him not, "ye sons of God;"
He raised you up, in His love for all,　　·
　And placed you over the worm and clod.

SELF-PRIDE.

Speak not with a soft and a silly pride
　Of the things you've done, both good and
　　true,
But think, as the world moves by your side,
　Of the many things that you should do.

INTELLECTUAL.

The lower life's station, the closer are
　　wrought
The walls of our soul's intellectual sphere,
And the higher we climb on the ladder of
　　thought,
The wider the arches of heaven appear.

HEREAFTER.

We mark the foot-prints coming out of dawn;
  We watch them till they fade away in
    night;
In faith we see them leading on and on,
  In other worlds more spiritually bright.

———————

HERETOFORE.

We mark the foot-prints coming out of dawn,
  And wonder why the light reveals no more.
Far back of life's mysterious curtain drawn,
  Are there no foot-prints on the heretofore?

GOD'S PLAN.

God knows much better than the man
  Why that has been or this should be;
Be hopeful then. His loving plan
  Was perfected for you and me.

PROCRASTINATION.

"To-morrow," says the sluggard, "I'll arise
  And do the work—to-day's too short and
      narrow."
The morning comes; he opes his drowsy
      eyes
And mutters still, "To-morrow."

FARTHER ON.

A little farther on and these defeats
  Which grieve us now will all be past and
      gone:
So all thro' life the hopeful heart repeats,
  "A little farther on."

BELATED KNOWLEDGE.

An old man told me once, "Life's fugitive
  Will never learn until his end is nigh;
And when he's found out how he ought to
      live,
  He's ready then to die."

DOWNCAST EYES.

The one with eyes upon the ground
  May tell you how the shadows lie,
But never of the beauties found
  Within the azure sky.

LOOK UP.

Come, place your eyes upon the skies,
  And fix your thoughts upon a star;
Then filled with Nature's promises,
  The shadows will be far.

THE ROGUE.

The rogue may shun the laws of man,
  And be a much respected creature
Among his fellows, but he can
  Not shun a single law of Nature.

THOSE I MEET.

When I see whom I please, and please those
    whom I see,
My life is a peace and a pleasure to me;
But when I go mix with the mixtion of men,
    I drop to the depth of despondency then.

ONLY A MAN.

I am only a man with a mannish plan,
    In a sinful world, with the worldly sin;
Here trudging along with my kin and clan,
    And fighting along (with myself) to win.

THE SHADOWS.

Those shadows in your heart, my love,
    Have object thoughts within the mind,
With just enough of light above
    To cast them where they lie outlined.

LOVE'S SUNSHINE.

Let that love divine and holy,
　Which the thoughts of life enroll,
Cast its squares of dreamy sunshine
　Thro' the windows of the soul.

FLOWERS OF LIFE.

Flowers plucked and pressed with love;
　Flowers plucked and pressed with strife:
Bookmarks, gathered as we rove
　In the winding walks of life.

HER TEARS.

She never tried to hide her smile
　Which filled with joy the many years;
But ah, how sad to me the while
　She tried so hard to hide her tears.

THE LOOKING-GLASS.

The looking-glass will tell the truth
  When e'er confronted for an interview,
Both to the aged and the youth—
  And that is more than many friends will do.

DECEPTION.

Ofttimes the needy will not beg from thee;
  Too manly they, to ask for charity;
While those who plenty have, and have to
      spare,
  Will beg with faces pitiful as prayer.

INVITE THE SUN.

If there be tears still lingering in thy heart,
  'Twere better they should flow till they are
      done;
If darkness trouble to thy soul impart,
  Go let it out, and then invite the sun.

BELIEF.

How gladly beats the heart of one
  Who builds a faith beyond to-day;
Who trusts in this: *Thy will be done*,
  And feels his soul is not of clay.

UNBELIEF.

How sadly beats the heart of one
  Who sees no farther than the mould,
And feels, when his dear loves are gone,
  That all is ended—in the cold.

EVOLUTION.

As brick by brick the wall is laid
  Until it meets the sky above,
So step by step our journey's made
  To Peace, to Purity, and Love.

6

PENTASTICHS.

1.

THOUGHTS.

These messengers are never checked
  By wind or weather, wave or rocks;
But in their magic feathers decked,
Thro' shade and sunshine they collect,
  And go and come in silent flocks.

2.

LIFE'S STORY.

This life is but a story read
By souls who can not see ahead,—
  Whose Author's wise and blessed aim,
  Is not to give His loving name,
Until the closing leaf is read.

82

3.

PURITY.

Every bloom and bursting bud
　　Holds a plea
　　For purity:—
Sweet commandment of our God,
　Sent alike to you and me.

—

4.

INSEPARABLE.

Verse and poet only part
　To rejoin as friends again;
What is written in the heart,
Must reveal a counterpart
　In the copy from the pen.

5.

SINKING.

———

Sinking:—a flaming light
　　Down thro' the western sky,
　　　While the columbine
　　　And the rose divine
　　Look up to say good-bye.

———

6.

RISING.

———

Rising:—a mellow light
　　Far in the orient gray,
　　　While the rose divine
　　　And the columbine
　　Look up to greet the day.

7.

ENVOY.

If I had a couch of the rosy clouds,
  And a pillow of airy light,
I would wrap myself in a twilight gown,
With the starry curtains of heaven dropped
  down,
  And dream of my God to-night.

V.

Verses.

VERSES.

THE GNOME.

Down in the depth of a mountain cave,
  Where the winds play "who-pee-do,"
        A gay gnome sits
        On the broken bits
  Of the topaz, peeping thro'
At the mystic light which is drifting in from
  a sky that is cold and blue.

And there with a cloak of the checkered
    light,
  And a harp of the straying wind,
        He plays and sings
        Of the many things
  Which flit thro' his jocund mind,
Nor feels for the grief of this outside world
    which his dreams have left behind.

ON ELFIN WATERS.

———

I knew Elfin Iho well;
    Elfin Iho well knew me;
So he led me in a dream
    To a magic brook and sea.

There it was, the Magic Brook,
    Like a winding strip of sky,
Where the pinks and "what-be-nots,"
    Bloomed and nodded sweetly by.

But instead of flowing down
    Thro' the land, as waters do,
It went gliding up the hill,
    Emptying into azure blue.

"Now," said Iho, "we will sail
    Seaward on its crystal tide."
So he launched a golden leaf,
    And we rigged it for our ride.

Silvery cobwebs formed our ropes,
  And our sail the gauzy wing
Of a butterfly, which caught
  Buoyantly the breath of spring.

Up we went towards the peak,
  Passing many a laughing rill,
Rounding many a curve and rock,
  As a bird would soar the hill.

Soon we reached the Magic Sea,
  Where the stars were on its floor,
And some broken bits of moon
  Lay strewn out along its shore.

By its brink a pier uprose,
  Built of amethyst and green,
Holding up a rainbow bridge,
  Arching out above the scene.

All its waves were twilight blue,
  By the zephyrs softly scrolled,
As we swiftly sailed away
  From its banks of sunset gold.

Overhead were fairy suns
  With a light as soft as snow,
While we watched our shadows glide
  Over starry shoals below.

When far out upon the wave,
  Out of sight of land and pier,
Iho stopped our leaf to rest,
  And said, "Listen! don't you hear?"

Out across the twilight tide
  Came a music soft as light;
This, he said, was Elfin bands
  Playing on the Isle of Night.

Then he told me that the bridge,
  Laid in gold and green and gray,
Was the pass-way over which
  Many went to hear them play.

"Oh," cried I, "let's sail to them."
  Iho smiled and laid his hand
On the golden rudder stem,
  Heading for the Elfin land.

Now the scene began to fade,
  While the music still flowed on;
Out I reached my hand—alas!
  Elf and leaf and sea were gone!

Up I jumped—"Ah, Iho's sea
  Must have sprung a-leak," I said;
And it had—The rain poured down
  On the shingles overhead!

EVENING ON THE FARM.

Sunset gilds the cotton-wood
    Where the leafy nests are many—
Homes which wrapped in quietude
    Have but little grief—if any.

By the pond the noisy geese
    Flop their wings and cry for trouble,
While the "chickies" scold for peace
    On the straw-ricks and the stubble.

Out upon the well-curb, puss
    Eyes the pup, that, crouched below her,
Barks and looks as mischievous
    As a woolly clown before her.

Now the puffing cattle come
    Up from pastures faintly sunny,
Where the bees are flying home
    With their stores of pilfered honey.

By the barn the pigs are all
    Quarreling over corn presented,
While their shadows on the wall
    Are as black and discontented.

At his door the pigeon sits,
    Smoothing down his breast of feathers,
While the swallow soars and flits
    With the stubble which she gathers.

Brush Grove, Iowa.

THE GROVE.

I.

Summer breezes fill the grove,
  Laden with the flowery breath
Of the prairie, green and gold—
  Which the winter puts to death.

II.

Snows of winter, white and cold,
  Winds as cutting as a knife,
Put a death within the grove—
  Which the summer filled with life.

Brush Grove, Iowa, 1884.

DROPS OF RAIN.

——

I.

Now the driven drops of rain
Rest a while
On a frowning window-pane,
Where the smile
Of a little child in-doors,
Saddens as her heart deplores
For the straying drops which cling
To the cold and glassy thing,
Till with sympathy and love,
For the wanderer from above,
She with fingers soft and thin
Takes them in.

II.

Let these driven thoughts of mine
          Rest awhile
On the window-lights divine
          Of the soul,
Till an angel watching there
In the dark and murky air,
Sees the straying hopes which grope
In life's cold and glassy scope,
And at Heaven's wise command,
She extends her loving hand,
And from out this world of sin
          Takes them in.

FINALE.

I.

The stars are spinning on their way.
  Low in the west the last faint line
  Of sunset dies about the pine
Which leans against the sinking day.

The twilight gathers—far and near
  I see the misty peaks of white,
  That shoulder all the sleeping night,
Which rests above the rolling sphere.

II.

The book is closed and laid away,
  While on its pages, black and white,
  There blink the stars of yesternight,
And sleeps the sun of yesterday.

Its fading pictures, once so fair,
  By Fancy's artful fingers wrought,
  Are now but glimmering ghosts of thought,
Which vanish in the viewless air.

Its hopes and aspirations raised,
　　As banners worked with rhymed device,
　　Seem now but barren crags of ice,
Where late the sun of courage blazed.

But hist!—I hear among its leaves
　　A dream—as quiet as a mouse—
　　A dream which raids the dreamer's house,
Where busy Fancy sits and weaves

A garment from the threads of light,
　　Which warm the planets on their march—
　　A garment donned by heaven's arch,
And buttoned with the stars of night.

Oh linger, Hope, betwixt the gray
　　Of leaves, where Fancy paints her dreams—
　　The dreams which die ere morning beams,
And sleep forgotten by the day.

www.ingramcontent.com/pod-product-compliance
Lightning Source LLC
Chambersburg PA
CBHW032204010726
47493CB00008BA/2818